Puffin Books

THE STORY OF FERDINAND

In Spain most self-respecting young bulls want
more than anything else to be picked to fight at the
bull fights in the great arenas. *But not Ferdinand.*

'Why don't you run and play with the other
little bulls and skip and butt your head?' his mother
asked. But Ferdinand preferred to sit under the
cork tree and smell the flowers . . .

This is the story of what happened when the five
grand men came to choose a fierce bull to fight
in the arena in Madrid, of how they chose Ferdinand,
and how . . .

You must read for yourself this funny and endearing
story about the nicest bull there ever was. All
young children will be sure to love Ferdinand,
whether the story is read to them or whether they
follow his magnificent adventure for themselves,
to its happy and satisfying conclusion where he sits
under the cork tree, 'smelling the flowers just quietly'.

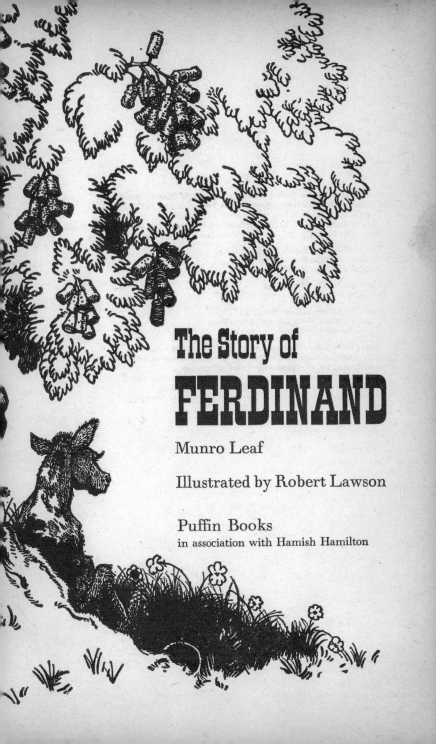

The Story of

FERDINAND

Munro Leaf

Illustrated by Robert Lawson

Puffin Books
in association with Hamish Hamilton

Puffin Books, Penguin Books Ltd, Harmondsworth, Middlesex, England
Penguin Books, 625 Madison Avenue, New York, New York 10022, U.S.A.
Penguin Books Australia Ltd, Ringwood, Victoria, Australia
Penguin Books Canada Ltd, 2801 John Street, Markham, Ontario, Canada L3R 1B4
Penguin Books (N.Z.) Ltd, 182–190 Wairau Road, Auckland 10, New Zealand

First published by Hamish Hamilton 1937
Published in Puffin Books 1967
Reprinted 1977, 1978, 1981

Copyright 1937 by Munro Leaf
All rights reserved

Made and printed in Great Britain by
Hazell Watson & Viney Ltd, Aylesbury, Bucks
Set in Monotype Walbaum

Once upon a time in Spain

there was a little bull and
his name was Ferdinand.

All the other little bulls he lived with would run and jump and butt their heads together, but not Ferdinand.

He liked to sit just quietly and smell the flowers.

He had a favourite spot out in the pasture under a cork tree.

It was his favourite tree
and he would sit in its
shade all day and smell
the flowers.

Sometimes his mother, who was a cow, would worry about him. She was afraid he would be lonely all by himself.

'Why don't you run and play with the other little bulls and skip and butt your head?' she would say.

But Ferdinand would shake his head. 'I like it better here where I can sit just quietly and smell the flowers.'

His mother saw that he was not lonely, and because she was an understanding mother, even though she was a cow, she let him just sit there and be happy.

As the years went by
Ferdinand grew and grew
until he was very big
and strong.

All the other bulls who had grown up with him in the same pasture would fight each other all day. They would butt each other and stick each other with their horns. What they wanted most of all was to be picked to fight at the bull fights in Madrid.

But not Ferdinand—he still liked to sit just quietly under the cork tree and smell the flowers.

One day five men came in
very funny hats to pick the
biggest, fastest, roughest bull
to fight in the bull fights
in Madrid.

All the other bulls ran around snorting and butting, leaping and jumping so the men would think that they were very very strong, and fierce, and pick them.

Ferdinand knew that they wouldn't pick him and he didn't care. So he went out to his favourite cork tree to sit down.

He didn't look where he was sitting and instead of sitting on the nice cool grass in the shade he sat on a bumble bee.

Well, if you were a bumble bee and a bull sat on you what would you do? You would sting him. And that is just what this bee did to Ferdinand.

Wow! Did it hurt! Ferdinand jumped up with a snort. He ran around puffing and snorting, butting and pawing the ground as if he were mad.

The five men saw him and they all shouted with joy. Here was the largest and fiercest bull of all. Just the one for the bull fights in Madrid!

So they took him away for
the bull fight day in a cart.

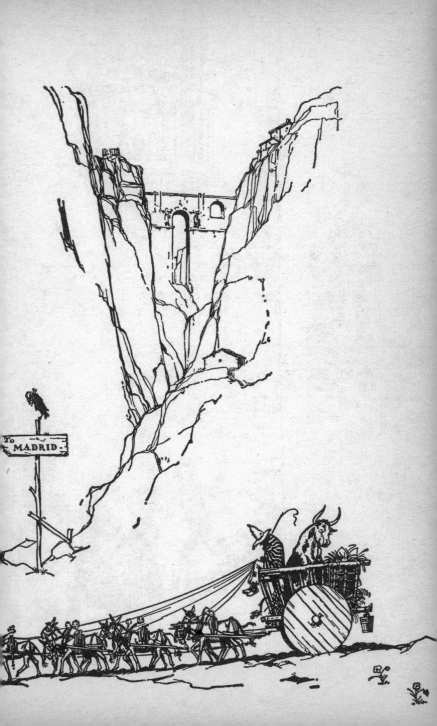

What a day it was! Flags
were flying, bands were
playing . . .

VINO

and all the lovely ladies had flowers in their hair.

They had a parade into the
bull ring.

First came the Banderilleros
with long sharp pins with
ribbons on them to stick in
the bull and make him
angry.

Next came the Picadores
who rode skinny horses and
they had long spears to
stick in the bull and make
him angrier.

Then came the Matador, the proudest of all—he thought he was very handsome, and bowed to the ladies. He had a red cape and a sword and was supposed to stick the bull last of all.

Then came the bull, and
you know who that was
don't you?

— FERDINAND.

They called him Ferdinand the Fierce and all the Banderilleros were afraid of him and the Picadores were afraid of him and the Matador was scared stiff.

Ferdinand ran to the middle of the ring and everyone shouted and clapped because they thought he was going to fight fiercely and butt and snort and stick his horns around.

But not Ferdinand. When he got to the middle of the ring he saw the flowers in all the lovely ladies' hair and he just sat down quietly and smelled.

He wouldn't fight and be fierce no matter what they did. He just sat and smelled. And the Banderilleros were angry and the Picadores were angrier and the Matador was so angry he cried because he couldn't show off with his cape and sword.

So they had to take
Ferdinand home.

And for all I know he is sitting there still, under his favourite cork tree, smelling the flowers just quietly.

He is very happy.

A list of other Young Puffins will be found on the
following pages. Most of them are collections of
self-contained stories and are therefore especially suitable
for reading aloud. They are also ideal for children who
have just started to read.

Celebrated anthologies of stories especially selected for each age group and tested in the classroom by the editors.

The Lost Merbaby and the Wishing Nut Tree

MARGARET AND MARY BAKER

Two fairy tales with a traditional basis, told with economy and charm. Both are accompanied by exquisite, lively silhouette drawings on every page.

Katy and the Nurgla

HARRY SECOMBE

Katy had the whole beach to herself, until an old, tired monster swam up to the very rock where she was sitting reading. Harry Secombe's first book for children has all the best ingredients in just the right proportions: a monster, a spaceship, adventure, humour and more than a touch of happy sadness.

Two Village Dinosaurs

PHYLLIS ARKLE

Two dinosaurs spell double trouble as Dino and Sauro trample their amiable way through the village, causing chaos and confusion on every side!

Brinsly's Dream

PETRONELLA BREINBURG

'Never be afraid. You're as good as the next man,' Brinsly told himself, and he threw himself heart and soul into getting his football team up to scratch for the big match.

Dinner at Alberta's

RUSSELL HOBAN

Arthur the crocodile has extremely bad manners - until he is invited to Alberta's for dinner.

The New Red Bike

SIMON WATSON

Sixteen short stories about a lively and logical small boy called Wallace, his nice parents, his daily adventures and occasional disgraces, all told with humour and understanding.

Hide Till Daytime

JOAN PHIPSON

The two children had been locked into the big department store by mistake at closing time, and whose were those prowling steps they could hear through the dark?

The Adventures of Sam Pig
Yours Ever, Sam Pig
Sam Pig Goes To The Seaside
Sam Pig Goes To Market
Sam Pig And Sally

ALISON UTTLEY

Collections of stories about Alison Uttley's best-loved creation, Sam Pig, and his farm animal friends.

The Dial-A-Story Book

H.E. TODD

Magic pops up in the strangest places when Bobby and Barbara Brewster are around! A collection of three stories, especially written for the British Telecom Bedtime Story service.

Saturday by Seven

PENELOPE FARMER

Peter should have been saving for a month to get the money needed to go camping with the Cubs. Now there is only one day left, and how can he possibly earn it in time?

The Worst Witch

JILL MURPHY

Mildred Hubble had a reputation for being the worst pupil in Miss Cackle's school for witches. So when things started to go wrong at the Hallowe'en celebrations, she was naturally at the centre of it all.

Mrs Pepperpot's Year

ALF PRØYSEN

'Goodness', said the little girl in hospital when she saw that the nice old lady who was tucking her in had suddenly shrunk to a few inches high, 'you must be Mrs Pepperpot!' 'Right first time,' said Mrs Pepperpot, 'and now it's your turn to help me.'

Matthew's Secret Surprises

TERESA VERSCHOYLE

Happy stories about a little boy exploring his new home, a cottage tucked away by the sea, with all its secrets and surprises. (*Original*)

Carrot Tops

JOAN WYATT

Fifteen stories of everyday events like making a jelly, growing a carrot-top garden, visiting Granny - all tinged with the make-believe that young children love.

Who is he?

His name is Smudge, and he's the mascot of the Junior
Puffin Club.

What is that?

It's a Club for children between 4 and 8 who are beginning to
discover and enjoy books for themselves.

How does it work?

On joining, members are sent a Club badge and Membership
Card, a sheet of stickers, and their first copy of the magazine,
The Egg, which is sent to them four times a year. As well as
stories, pictures, puzzles and things to make, there are
competitions to enter and, of course, news about new Puffins.

For details of cost and an application form, send a stamped
addressed envelope to:

*The Junior Puffin Club
Penguin Books Limited
Bath Road
Harmondsworth
Middlesex UB7 0DA*